MIDDLE AGE RAE

OF

FUCKING SUNSHINE

By Dani Brown

MorbidbookS.Wordpress.Com

'RAE'~Dani Brown~

Rae, her buck-tooth grin and rosy cheeks of middle age acne reflected winter sun. Straw-like blonde hair obscured by the veil and tiara she enjoyed parading around in. She walked past our window with sickening confidence oblivious to us and our weak tea.

Rae. Everything was always about Rae. Was she a princess today, or was she a bride? Did she know or care? Did it even matter? We wished we could be that delusional and walk around with an air of not giving a damn...

'RAE'~Dani Brown~

ONE

Rae never realised marriage is for life and not just for two weeks. She also never realised grown women shouldn't play dress up or not in public at least. That sort of thing should be saved for the bedroom and cos-play conventions.

Rae is the reason why the rest of us aren't allowed to make that life-long commitment. Her actions made the rest of us too stupid to understand the meaning of marriage regardless of how high our I.Qs might be. We know exactly what marriage entails. It is a commitment some of us are desperate to have but we will never know the joys of walking down the aisle.

Some of us had our children taken away because Rae drowned her offspring in bleach, piss and after-birth. We would have never done something so evil and sick. Some of us choose not to reproduce so we wouldn't learn the heartache of having children taken at birth naked and covered in blood. Rae's children were never taken away; even after she drowned the first two within minutes of pushing them out.

Rae. None of us have a job because of her. We exist on welfare payments and charity. No one wants to give someone who had a traumatic start to life a job in case they go bat-shit crazy. They think we might lock everyone in a parking garage and seal up all the vents, except the one used to pump in cyanide gas and wait for someone to try to ram the barricaded doors as people switch on their cars and the cyanide mixes with exhaust. Society thinks the rest of us will do that. Even after the unfortunate fume-filled demise of her colleagues that she watched on CCTV, Rae was able to find a new job. She kept her job after she posted the footage online with detailed plans of how she was going to repeat it on her new colleagues.

Instead of filling our days with meaningful work we fill our days with weak tea and the support group for those whose lives have been so thoroughly destroyed by Rae there are no longer any pieces to pick up. They've been shattered to dust. Nothing can help us now. Not even Rae's death would help, although that would be nice, especially if it was slow and painful beyond all description.

We sit around and talk about ways to convince society and the authorities and pretty much everyone that none of us are anything like Rae the Super Life Destroying Villianairess with a little touch of rat (at least on her face). No one ever believes us no matter how much we put into our efforts. We have to give more of ourselves to each thing we do due to abuse from so long ago as it is without Rae and her antics making all former victims (the press's words) come across as damaged goods.

Rae has stacked up more two week marriages than the mutants in the forest have fingers and toes to count them on. But her marriages affect them too. Due to Rae, the mutants in the forest don't have their marriages recognised by the government. In some cases, husband and wife are separated by the state just because they have extra fingers and toes and forked tongues and live in the trees. Rae has never lived in a tree; princesses don't like trees unless there are MDF castles in them, but those in authority don't care.

She is known to social services yet Rae can continue destroying everyone's life in a ripple, like throwing a stone into still water. Even people who have never met her and don't even know of her existence have their lives ruined by her.

We ladies in our support group can't live life as we choose. We can't do anything except sit around and drink weak tea with UHT milk. Some think we shouldn't be trusted with the kettle and mugs. They vow to take them off us. We would tell them where they can stick the kettle and mugs but we had our toaster taken away last year when some social worker who never met any of us decided that one or more of us might stick a fork in it (we're only allowed plastic sporks and it has always been that way). The paranoia of losing our tea is very real. It is, rather literally, all we have left – even the clothes on our backs are in the process of disintegration and we don't know when we'll be allowed new ones.

Rae is the local jiz-recycling plant. Society thinks every other person who has been at the receiving end of a violent sexual assault is always interested in more. Most of us here in the support group can testify that statement is false but no one listens to us. On the rare occasion when someone does, the absolute opposite of what we say is recorded.

Last week Sally won a trip to the cinema from the radio station. She was taken in the toilets by three of the employees. This week she has to sit on one of those inflatable doughnut cushions popular with haemorrhoid suffers. Rae is a giant bleeding haemorrhoid blocking the anus of our lives but there is no doughnut ring cushion to make sitting down any less painful. Sally has the underlying smell of stale popcorn about her still, underneath the combined odours of piss and shit.

'RAE'~Dani Brown~

We've reached the end of our tolerance of doing nothing except sitting around in our support group drinking weak tea and exchanging medications and Rae-related horror stories. We're going to do something about Rae. It is about the only thing we can do to benefit humanity.

We've had enough of being told we don't know what marriage means because our lives bore some slight resemblance to Rae's or we had one thing in common with her – notice the past tense. It is always the past and never the present or the future. In our support group it is the distant past of our miserable existences. But the authorities and society don't care. Once you've been bathed in Rae's filth there is no bleach strong enough to cleanse it away.

Rae shouldn't be allowed to continue in her existence. None of us would hurt our children but we aren't allowed to know their post-adoptive names. Or even the area of the country they are living in. It isn't our fault Rae took the decision to drown everything she has ever let fall out of her gaping vagina (there was no pushing involved there).

We've been pushed too far by Rae and the people who agree to marry her with the belief that this time she has changed and the nuptials will last beyond two weeks. She is never going to change. She doesn't have it in her. And she doesn't think she does anything wrong; it is everyone else with the problem.

She has left behind a trail of very broken people (and drowned infants and gassed colleagues). All those husbands and wives and their partners before she snatched them away in the ripples of devastation.

More than one of her spouses had a child or two from a previous relationship that she drowned in her pool (compensation payment). Every life those children touched has now been destroyed. How Rae and her spouse were awarded custody instead of the child's other parent is beyond our comprehension, especially with her record of murdering children.

All those families she broke apart when she gassed her work colleagues with cyanide and exhaust fumes. She carried on as if nothing was wrong without a care for the children of those people she killed or their partners, parents or twenty cats. Everyone had someone in their lives, no matter how miserable, which cared about them – now they're left tending gravesides and shedding their pointless tears into urns.

Rae had this need to cause drama wherever she goes. Her constant desire to be the centre of attention causes those who bear witness or worse, involved in one way or another a mountain of trauma that lasts for many years if they're lucky enough to make it out alive. Without the drama of other people's wrecked lives she will die from malnourishment.

Let's not forget about us in our support group with our weak tea. We take little sips and complain about all the negative ways Rae impacted our lives until it is time to go back to our dilapidated homes.

'RAE' ~Dani Brown~

We repeat every weekday, except bank holidays. We've done it every weekday for years. We have nothing else to do and nowhere else to go.

Every now and then a new member joins. Sometimes the new member had her life recently ruined by Rae but often times she had her life destroyed years ago and only now found out about us by wandering into the community centre during bad weather. We aren't publicised, but then again, neither is the International Sheep Hoarders Association North West England and Northern Wales Branch (they meet in the community centre too).

The younger members never last long. They don't believe their lives are forever ruined. They try to pick up the pieces. Too many fall through their fingers because Rae gave them proverbial carpal tunnel. They try again and again until all the pieces have dissolved into dust and blown away on a Rae-scented wind ripe with an airborne mutation of the herpes virus.

'RAE'~Dani Brown~

TWO

We're going to take action, once we decide what that action is going to be. Rae can't continue to wreak havoc where-ever she spreads her legs. It comes down to us. We're the only people who really know what Rae is capable of. It is rather obvious all the bad in the world has her stink on it but the people remain oblivious.

Sally thinks we should violate her anus with a razor wire wrapped cricket bat. The support group shot this suggestion down; Rae's anus holds the world's record for loosest; she wouldn't feel a cricket bat even if we put razor wire dipped in chilli oil around it. We'll let Sally have a cricket bat and razor wire so she can relieve her anger and have her vengeance for the cinema incident.

We require an idea that will make her suffer. It should take away parts of her soul, over a shorter timespan than how we were separated from ours. It needs to always be a reminder of us and our weak tea. We aren't allowed the types of films, books and games where we could draw influence. Weak tea isn't the best creativity or intellect driver but some arsehole thought it a good idea to make LSD illegal. If this butt-wipe knew of Rae, LSD would be available from the supermarket right next to children's cough formula and sniper rifles.

Debbie suggested we kidnap her. Once Rae is in our custody we should drug to make her more docile. That's the next logical step. Between us we're on enough meds to open a small chemist. But we don't want her too docile; she might not realise anything is happening to her and that would be pure insanity on our part. Contrary to popular belief, we aren't insane.

Lisa thinks if we hold Rae's head in a tank of pedicure fish with flexi-straws shoved up her nostrils it will be like waterboarding but with fish acting like the prize in a box of cereal. She spewed the suggestion out quickly with much mumbling. It took a few moments for it to translate in our heads. It showed such brilliance from one who hardly spoke at all. We would have been curious to know what else Lisa keeps behind those sunken eyes of her's but the excessive meds clouded our thoughts and we required all our brain power to form a plan.

We agreed that Rae's wrists and ankles required binding for successful waterboarding. The festering water could make the drugs wear off and she is a beast of a troll-like woman with the strength to overpower any of us with ease.

We should use the rusty razor wire that Lucy stole from the industrial estate two weeks ago. We need to put it to use before someone discovers it and takes it away. The kleptomaniacs might steal it and hold it to ransom. But it isn't them taking it that we're worried about. If someone in authority finds it, we may lose our weak tea forever.

With the basic formation of a plan we needed a fish tank filled with little flesh eating fishes. We weren't allowed pets. We were deemed too immature to be entrusted with keeping something else alive.

None of our homes even had the most basic of potted plants because, apparently, plants have feelings too.

Not so long ago, even the high-end spa-style nail salons offered fish pedicures in their windows. A tacky High Street nail bar in an area with high unemployment should have at least one fish tank filled with little fish that feast on dead skin straight off the bloated feet of customers. There are at least five of them in the town centre alone.

It has been said that anything unfortunate enough to fall from Rae's vagina was drowned a short while later by its mother. Maybe the sensation of being held under water will result in a sudden attack of conscious (unlikely) or post-traumatic stress (we can only hope). If the faces of her murdered infants flash before her eyes and she bursts into tears she might be heard so we should gag her with Sally's crusty underpants.

Sally liked the idea. Her lacy pound shop panties were splattered with blood and pus and smelled strongly of urine and shit because it hurt to wipe with the cheap scratchy toilet paper provided by the community centre. She didn't have enough spare change to buy more than three pairs of pants and she was only allowed to do laundry once every other Wednesday so she wore her underpants for days at a time.

Sally was in no condition to aide in the theft of a fish tank. She stayed behind to ensure there would be plenty of weak tea upon our return. It pained her to walk and it pained her to sit down but she had those teas waiting for us. She even found a pack of biscuits. They were a bit soft but it didn't matter. Biscuits in any state of freshness were a rare luxury. Some of us hadn't tasted them since our lives were good.

THREE

We put the fish tank in the middle of our weak tea room without spilling anymore festering water down ourselves. The other support groups didn't offer their assistance. The choice they made instead, to gawk as we struggled past their rooms was typical of the apathy of lives destroyed or controlled by one aspect.

A lot of water spilled when we lifted it out of the nail salon. That meant the tiles in the salon were slippery and we left a trail of water down the High Street but the floor in the community centre remained dry – that was the important thing. Any sign of non-conforming and we'd be labelled as even more damaged and could lose our privilege to the community centre.

Fish tanks are heavy, made more so, due to our weakened state from poor diet. The dead and dying fish didn't have much weight but the water did, until we spilled most of it leaving the salon.

The kleptomaniacs have jugs in their treasure chest of stolen goodies. We had no doubt that if we asked one would be made available for our usage with no questions and we were right. We didn't really want to add fresh water but we didn't want any more fish to die. They needed to be alive to swim into Rae's ear canals.

We took the tank with an ease that surprised us all. For once, something seemed to be going in our favour. Life was never that easy for any of us. We were anxious about when the theft would catch up to us.

It was opening hours for the salon so the doors were unlocked but no one was inside and the lights weren't on. The lack of customers and staff didn't become curious until we returned to the community centre. But not curious enough to waste precious brain power contemplating. Our brain power was needed in trying to decide what to do next.

Edie used to keep fish in ponds and tanks before Rae wrecked her life. She said that without any filtration the fish would suffocate in their own filth. We knew we would have to kidnap Rae before the fish could perish. At the nail bar it wasn't hooked up to any pumps or filtration devices. The creatures were probably seen as disposable to the salon as other peoples' lives are to Rae.

The cleaners were addicted to heroin; they would never notice the fish tank – they were only trusted with watered down cheap disinfectant (which they probably still tried to get a buzz from). We were only left with hope that no one of importance would peek through the re-enforced glass window of our door. Our weak tea was at risk. We sweated with the knowledge but something had to be done about Rae. No one less damaged was doing anything about her.

We wouldn't be damaged if Rae didn't exist. Society awarded us the label, we didn't consent to it. Rae is the damaged one. In turn, Rae damaged us but not beyond repair until the authorities got a hold of us. They said the word, "broken" and took away everything we had worked towards and held dear.

Tomorrow we will track down Rae for a date with the fishes (before they all die). We have a general idea of her movements. We don't stalk her

'RAE'~Dani Brown~

exactly, but it is always a good idea to keep track of the one who ruined a life or many lives before they can strike again.

After our final cups of weak tea we filed into the toilets – both male and female because there aren't any men in our support group and we're always the last one to leave the community centre each evening. The recovering chocoholics leave half an hour before us. They have pleasant homes with nice families and pets and chocolate stashed beneath the floorboards to get back to.

Sally cried out with enough pain to shake the cold air strong with the scent of watered down disinfectant and cheap air freshener. The sound was more like a cat being gang-banged by much larger cats than something from a woman's throat. Urine burnt when it hit torn and battered skin. She passed around pictures of her injuries so each and every one of us knew what urine and shit were splashing against. It was amazing waste could pass the purple swelling.

The doctors gave her the minimum of treatments. The event was a name a lifestyle choice by the nurses and hospital social worker. They said she was over-reacting. They sent her for a psychological evaluation when she denied it and asked for better treatment with some painkillers. She was threatened with being struck off for asking for a second opinion. She couldn't even walk the day after her trip to the cinema. We had to do our best to carry her to the community centre when Debbie found her passed out on the pavement. We all went home with sore backs that night. None of us bothered seeing a doctor as apparently our backs didn't hurt; we were simply seeking attention and wasting time.

Once we finished we switched off the lights and locked the door, like we do every evening. The community centre actually trusts us with a set of keys, which is really kind of them. Not many people trust damaged goods with anything. It is a big responsibility and the only one we have. We share it.

Sally took the keys home with her. Letting her have the keys since the unfortunate incident in the cinema has given her a sense of purpose and reason to live, especially as the police refused to take a statement believing she was up for it regardless of how many times she said she wasn't. How they drew such a conclusion is beyond our reasoning. We suspect they might be both lazy and stupid.

FOUR

We say our goodbyes in the car park. As no employers will trust us enough to give any of us a job and the Department for Work and Pensions state none of us qualify for disability none of us have the luxury of a car. There isn't much point to the community centre having a car park. No one in any of the support groups has a car. Even members of support groups that aren't deemed too damaged to drive and be in employment. Cars are expensive and becoming a rare luxury.

Mutant weeds that can withstand the cold sprout up from cracks in the pavement fed off the tears of the support groups. We avoid the weeds. It is only a matter of time before Rae is able to feed her drowned babies to them. The vines have teeth to wrap around our ankles and snare our pound shop tights. No one fancies being dragged across the car park by the plant life.

Our homes were in different directions. We walked off alone in our torn and dirty clothes each evening. Rush hour bus routes don't want to sell the likes of us a ticket. Too many other passengers complained even though our clothes are no worse than anyone else's' in this god-forsaken town.

The nights were long and dark and it was only half past five. Bright winter sunshine was unknown this far north, but the wind wasn't. The wind was capable of penetrating every hole in our clothes with an evil intelligence that a warm coat would sheltered us from. But new warm coats weren't for the likes of us.

'RAE'~Dani Brown~

People avoided eye contact. People avoided us in general. The locals think we're damaged goods and ready to herd them into an underground car park and gas them at the slightest provocation. The locals actually are damaged; otherwise they would escape this place. If they hadn't drowned their brains in cheap cider and inbreeding they might think to gas their neighbours.

People shuffled to where they needed to be; walking was something that couldn't be done with high levels of moonshine and anti-depressants corrupting the body. We were certain the forgotten butt-plugs and pieces of toilet paper didn't help in this regard. Neither did the piles and herpes, the latter spread by Rae to at least half of the town's population.

We couldn't see who lurked in the shadows. We don't know what their intentions or relation to Rae would be. We must assume, if they are capable of coherent thought then they've either been fucked or fucked over by Rae and therefore a sworn enemy (even the ones who fall into the fucked over category).

Rae could be sucking some random guy's cock while she takes it up the arse behind a dying evergreen to pass the time while we say our goodbyes. She might want to stalk us one by one and tie us up in sacks to use as piñatas on her next hen night. The shuffling inbreds about town would ignore our screams for help if they even noticed at all. It doesn't seem likely that they would.

Some of us live in homes with staff monitoring the doors and only are allowed out in the day. Even when we arrive back battered and bruised with pus seeping out of vaginas social workers put it down to "lifestyle choice" despite our insistence that it isn't. Raped, attacked, unemployed, unmarried and without our children due to Rae most certainly is not a lifestyle choice but no one ever listened to damaged goods. Damaged goods lacked the capacity to think. These social workers scrapped third class degrees with cheat sheets and external tutors so they know these things better than the survivors do.

We don't have opinions or even a say in what happens to us. We aren't allowed either. We've been too badly damaged. But not damaged badly enough for disability. We have to sign on fortnightly for our benefits to go into a bank account we have no control over.

Text messages assured each other we made it to our cold homes without incident. We were only allowed a small amount of credit on our phones each month so the one text message was all each of us could send. It worked out well though; Sally would text Debbie who would then text Lisa saying she and Sally arrived home safely. It kept going like that until the last person had a text. She would then text Sally. If Sally didn't hear from her within an hour then the authorities would be notified but they never sent out a search party. We would have to trust that these incidents were at least documented but we kept proof of our troubles in case they weren't. The proof will serve our defence if this incident of doling out justice reaches court; due to how badly damaged society views us, we have classed that happening as doubtful. We'll be separated and thrown into the lunatic asylum without a trial because we can't understand proceedings. It doesn't occur to social workers that most people require a law degree to understand the specifics of Her Majesty's justice.

FIVE

We felt safer making our way back to the community centre the next morning in the dull winter light, but daylight only offered a false sense of security — Rae's supporters were known to attack regardless of how much light was in the sky. The doors were already unlocked; each support group is given a set of keys.

The others may have been curious about the fish tank but not curious enough to take it. It appeared even the kleptomaniacs didn't want a tank of dying fish. It occurred to us they might fancy the challenge of taking it while we occupied the room.

More fish floated on top of the festering water than what was there the night before. We didn't plan to scoop them out before ducking Rae's head in. We anticipated Rae inhaling at least one through the gap left by the straws inserted into her nostrils. She had exceptionally large nostrils. They looked out of place, even on a nose of that size.

We would prefer she swallowed the fish that have been dead for a few days or more and have started the decomposition process. But those have sunk to the bottom. Therefore we will scoop them out and put them in a glass for her to drink with some festering water. We wished we were allowed a blender.

We needed to lure Rae to our support group, or forcibly take her from the street. Either would work. We were all intelligent enough to realise there would be punishment even if society didn't give us all the credit. We made the decision and if anyone or anything was to blame it was Rae. Frustration at our treatment due to Rae's behaviour coursed through our veins all hours of the lonely days and nights.

Promises of weak tea would never be enough to tempt Rae. Her employment and lack of state interference allowed her normal strength hot drinks. If only there were some penises in our group but men weren't as negatively impacted by her behaviour. Society saw fit to ban us from the sex shop so even if we had the money we couldn't lure her with a rubber cock. When the mood takes her she is partial to a spot of carpet munching according to the rumours. We have no way of finding out if there is any truth in them even with the internet. All Rae's social networking profiles are set to private, probably because she has left a massive tidal wave of destruction in her wake and people still allowed use of the internet would send her abuse. We weren't allowed internet access. Social workers took it away and said we had no need to use it and wouldn't understand if we did. The only thing we didn't understand was the statement saying we wouldn't understand.

SIX

Sally limped in late with her doughnut shaped inflatable ring. The keys jingled in her pocket, the only version of "Jingle Bells" that would ever be allowed to us. She looked worse than she was when we said our goodbyes. Her illness is down to the cinema staff thinking because Rae likes a forcible quickie in the toilet Sally does too. Sally doesn't. And she never has.

Her skin was pale except where bright red splotches kept boils hidden. The pus oozing out of the mountains indicated they had started the process of violent explosion sometime in the night. There were still more to erupt. Sally didn't seem to notice. They were the least of her worries and pains.

A film of milk-white mucus lined Sally's eyes like cataracts. It wasn't there the night before. She couldn't focus. It pained her to turn her head in the direction of a voice.

Those of us seated closest to her could feel the heat radiating off her like a mini star in the room. She didn't melt the plastic of the seat. It wouldn't have surprised us if it started to bubble.

She didn't smell too pleasant either – not even the decaying fish in the tank masked it. We weren't allowed Febreze incase we got high from it (or left it lying around where the junkie cleaners might find it). Perfume even from the discount shops was far outside our price range. We contemplated going to the kleptomaniacs for something to disguise the odour but we didn't want to offend Sally.

Sally was confused. She knew where she was a minute ago but not anymore. If she forgot everything due to the delirium it would have been a blessing. Delirium was unreliable and in this case, we thought it might prove fatal.

Sally obviously required intense medical attention but an ambulance would never be sent out to the community centre. They only come here if someone has gone mad. We contemplated phoning anyways and claiming someone's forked tongue danced across the windows and their lips slurped dried pigeon shit from the frames. Sally didn't have to be the window-licker. A man could be doing it, outside getting frostbite on his dick because he forgot to dress himself. The paramedics would listen to the operator rather than their medical expertise and Sally wouldn't be looked at during the search for this crazed naked window-licker, even with the heat radiating off her and the mucus on her eyes crusting over. If they did glance her way she'd end up spending the night in psychiatric care rather than intensive care. She could die there. Doctors ignore their years of work in the profession to condemn the likes of us. Somehow, Rae even affects that and their common sense.

One of us died of cancer last year. The symptoms were dismissed as an eating disorder over and over again by numerous doctors. Tabby collapsed right here in this room. We phoned an ambulance but she was dead and going cold by the time it arrived hours later. We had to wait for the police to come before the ambulance would even be sent out. We weren't allowed to go to the funeral, as the ones in authority don't think we can comprehend death.

Sally lives closer than the rest of us but her anus and vagina are going to take weeks to heal. Walking the short distance to the community centre each day has been taking its toll. It has only served to make matters worse. She should have been allowed the luxury of staying at home in bed for a week while the worse of the injuries were given a chance to heal. But such luxuries are denied to us. All of us, regardless of the situation.

The latest pictures make it look like the swelling has fused all her holes shut. Putting one foot in front of the other over and over again must tear apart the fused skin repeatedly and result new bruises with each step. We didn't hug her. The additional heat would have caused her blood to boil but we wanted to. We wanted to offer our love and comfort to Sally.

The accommodation she lived in kicked her out every day even though she clearly was in a physical state indicating she should've been on hospital bed pumped full of antibiotics and sedated to the next dimension. The staff where she lived, however, followed their tick boxes and Sally didn't tick enough of them to qualify as ill.

Sally was in no fit state to help think of ways to lure Rae to us. She didn't look capable of any form of coherent thought or staying conscious for much longer.

Lucy might have some paracetamol – she's like a walking chemist. She might even have something stronger for Sally to take her away to the land of unicorns and fluffy bunny-rabbits and cotton-candy skies. We weren't sure if Sally was going to make through the day. The dark thought of another funeral we'd be barred from attending danced in front of our minds but we didn't voice it; we didn't want Sally to give up.

SEVEN

Luring Rae required precision and planning combined with an awful lot of skill. Middle age women on a serious amount of medications who spend their weekdays in a support group with mugs of weak tea have an awful lot of time on their hands to plot these things when meds don't cloud the brain waves.

We wanted to be good friends and stay with Sally but we knew only one of us could stay. The best way to help Sally was to bring back a bound and gagged Rae while she was still somewhere within the realms of consciousness.

We left Sally slumped in her chair; our collective body heat wasn't helping. We went to examine the fish, the sooner we did all the dull tasks the higher the chances of Sally having life when we arrived back with Rae. Our medication-aided theory was if Sally witnessed Rae paying her dues, then she would come back to us and the swelling and infection would go down.

On a more practical note, we felt that at least twenty-five per cent of the fish needed to be alive when we dunk Rae's head. We couldn't predict how much longer the live ones would remain that way. Dead fish were going to serve their purpose, nothing goes to waste with us, but we wanted Rae to feel their attempts to swim past the straws into her nostrils and enter her ear canals.

We made Sally as comfortable as possible while Lisa took out her diary which kept notes on Rae's movements (in case the medication removed these things from our memories). It was sad; especially this close to justice, but Sally didn't seem to acknowledge us. Each passing second brought her closer to the pearly gates.

That woman (of sorts) ruined our lives so it is only right that we engage in a spot of mild stalking, not even the most paranoid person could get away with calling Lisa's diary actual stalking. We did like to have some warning of when she might strike one of us down. Each one of us contributed every time we saw Rae some place new. Then we went back the next day to see if she was there again. If she was, it earned an entry. The authorities never looked it at it; social workers convinced themselves we know only the most basic of words and can't form these into sentences. Why would they want to look at the rambling gibberish of a group of illiterates?

Lisa turned the pages of the diary until she found Rae's usual movements that day of the week for late winter. Rae's movements change with the seasons. She would often indulge in full nudity outdoor orgies in the summer but doesn't like the ice-cutting effect winter has on her nipples or the sweat pouring off dozens of bodies and dripping onto her only to freeze.

Rae was most likely to be found sucking off some random guy in the alley behind the chip shop. Her partner of the week (not her latest husband) would watch with an oversized butt-plug jammed so far up his arse he couldn't walk right. With a cock in her mouth she would have no reason to disrobe and risk the freezing air dancing around her pasty flesh.

Rae offered herself for free, if her lover didn't mind risking herpes. She was available to anyone but her preferred companions had families. She would film the acts and post them to the partner's (or partners) families and bosses.

She was known to take offense to those who tried to put a paper bag over her head. She should consider sucking off a plastic surgeon in exchange for free cosmetic procedures. That would render the paper bag unneeded if she found one with enough talents.

After her alleyway activities Rae was normally to be found sampling vibrators in the sex shop dressing room. Under normal circumstances she puts them back on the display without even wiping them. The staff hated it. No one is meant to sample the toys but Rae is above the law. Each vibrator she shoves up herself has to be thrown out, if her vaginal slime didn't dissolve it. The staff kept a box of gloves behind the counter for this very reason. They tried banning her but she cried "discrimination".

A trip to the sexual health clinic then follows. Antibiotics were no longer effective against the strains of gonorrhoea, very much in the plural sense, so she received experimental injections. Her outward appearance indicts second stage syphilis so she could be receiving treatment for that as well. The outbreak of explosive lip-herpes can't be treated with normal cold sore creams and anti-virals – it was just too exotic of a strain. She's a dream for a doctor specialising in experimental venereal disease treatments; apart from the viewing of her gapping blue vagina.

Sometime between her busy schedule of picking up more diseases and treating the ones she already had she her typical behaviour included making a display of not showing up for work or phoning in feigning illness (of which she had enough but only of the sexual kind). It didn't occur to Rae to show up on time or every day she was scheduled to. If any of us had the privilege of employment we would always go in unless desperate illness kept us away.

EIGHT

We planned to strike while she was occupied in the sexual health clinic. We planned to surround the building and lay in wait. There's a possibility she will offer the doctor a quickie without a condom. He studied sexually transmitted diseases most of his life but has never experienced any first hand and would like to do so. He had the curiosity of a cat and Rae had the only known case of 'blue waffle'. He felt he had to put his dick in it. That could delay the inevitable but we had the patience. We didn't mind waiting a few extra minutes for Rae to receive justice.

She won't be expecting us. She thinks everyone loves her. She doesn't care that she has left behind destruction everywhere she has so much as breathed. Her skewed vision of the reality she created for those unfortunate enough to come into contact with her would prove her undoing. She couldn't comprehend the damage, or the people left behind and their desire for harm to find her. Her karma credits had run out. She wouldn't find out until she exits the clinic.

Lucy rummaged in her bag for painkilling fever reducers. Unlike Rae, we had this little thing called empathy. We couldn't leave Sally in excruciating pain.

Sally looked worse with each passing minute. It didn't seem right to leave her by herself. The authorities would have accused her of faking and forced us to leave her. They wouldn't have allowed her a fever reducer. Someone would need to stay behind to look after her. If her fever climbed any higher she would need cold water to be placed on her forehead. It was the only right thing to do. And we cared. No one believes us, but we did.

NINE

With the kettle boiled for a second and final cup of weak tea we sat around and drank it like we do every day. We sat in near silence listening to Sally struggle for breath beneath her spreading infection and focusing on our own thoughts. On a normal day we sit and talk about how Rae ruined our lives and wipe away the drool that escapes our medicated lips with our grubby sleeves. Sometimes the stories are repeats. Sometimes we have some new horror to add. A lifetime of chatting won't cure us of all the evils Rae inflicted upon us.

We planned to leave just before mid-day, all except Sally and her inflatable doughnut ring haemorrhoid cushion and someone to look after her. Sally would have liked to join us but she didn't know who she was or where she was. We don't think she was beyond pain at that point.

We should have been able to draw straws to decide who remained behind but one of the other support groups stole them. Most likely the kleptomaniacs but sometimes the sheep hoarders like to play pranks so they could have taken them assuming us ladies with our weak tea would storm out of our room in search of the kleptomaniacs and our missing straws – possibly picking up rolling pins on the way (we would have to steal these rolling pins from the kleptomaniacs).

We had to have straws for our plan to work. We plan on picking up some on our way to kidnapping Rae. She needs to be able to breathe under water. Drowning her right away just won't do.

TEN

In Lucy's bag lived items beyond measure. She had everything except straws and fresh underpants for Sally. Her house was burgled many years ago at the start of her Rae-induced decline. She couldn't afford a decent security system even though she had a job. Once her house was broken into she lost not just her television but everything else she has worked for. The person responsible was let off with a slap on the wrist while she was blamed for the entire thing all because Rae was in court two weeks before for burglary and claimed it was because houses didn't have decent security systems. Lucy lost her job when she complained that she couldn't afford a security system. She has a lot of upper body strength to carry that bag around with her everywhere, not even the excessive medication took that away.

She dumped the entire contents onto the floor. Stuff scattered everywhere; most of it came to rest in the dust bunnies in the far corners of the room.

There weren't any straws, not even twenty-five year old ones from various fast food outlets. However we found a set of role playing dice. We needed one that had a number for each of us, minus Sally.

We were sure to take our medications every day on schedule leading up to our planned kidnap of Rae. We didn't want our bad state of mind to be blamed for the events but thinking clearly with medication induced brain fog was difficult. We needed to devise a way in which the dice would decide who would stay.

Lucy rummages through her dice until she comes up with one that has a side for each of us, minus Sally. Lucy is number one. To her right is number two, until we are all assigned numbers. Then she rolled. The dice landed in the centre of the floor just missing the fish tank. It bounced a few times. We all lean over to watch it, except Sally – yesterday leaning hurt her battered anus and vagina, she didn't seem aware of us, the dice or the room.

It landed on number four – Maria. She tried not to look too disappointed. No one wanted to hurt Sally's feelings but she failed miserably. Sally was a bit too feverish to notice. But her feelings would have been hurt if she had.

We had two hours before it would be time to go Two hours to sit around and nurse weak tea. We couldn't drink too much; it wouldn't serve if one of us was to piss in our pants, apart from the embarrassment, we lacked clean ones. There were some Tena Lady Discreet in the toilets but if all of us took one then the weak bladder support group would notice them as missing and suspicion might pass our way while we're making Rae pay for everything she has taken away from us, and then, she too would be taken away.

Lucy rummaged through her belongings scattered all over the dusty floor. She was looking for something, hopefully chloroform. It is unlikely that Rae had any immunity to it but Sarah purchased heroin from the drug dealer she was housed with just in case the chloroform wasn't effective. Lucy had a clean syringe and needle as well as a handkerchief in her pile of stuff from her bag. We weren't concerned about Rae receiving hepatitis with her heroin but we didn't want to accidently inject ourselves with hepatitis.

The minutes ticked by, each of us lost in our own thoughts. Memories of the past and anticipation of an afternoon to be spent dishing out justice.

The minutes became an hour. We still had another to go if we were to wrap Rae in a giant potato sack behind the STD clinic and bring her to our support group. It was so quiet we were able to hear the weak tea passing through our systems.

We decided to eat something to provide some strength for our task. The community centre didn't have a kitchen so two of us went out to get pre-packaged sandwiches. They weren't very appetising but they were all we could afford (Rae's fault) and we picked up some flexi-straws while we were in the shop.

Sally needed to eat something. Sally really required a feeding tube. We pulled apart half a sandwich for her and put it in her mouth but it fell out and down her chin mixed with salvia. She needed a doctor but due to Rae's phantom symptoms none would believe Sally even with all the signs of a nasty infection as a consequence of a violent sexual assault.

Rae needed to be force fed yellow custard whilst viewing pus leaking from Sally's wounds. If we can be confident it would result in no distress for Sally we can even squeeze some out and into Rae's custard. She probably has enough to make an entire dessert but harvesting it was likely to land her in a coffin.

Rae required a lot to be done to her to make up for the years of upset and ruin. An hour to think of what to do with her after her date with the fishes should have left us with plenty of ideas but medication zombification induces slowed thoughts and slurred speech.

Some of us had waterfalls of tears from two hours trapped within our own thoughts when it was time for a pre-kidnapping trip to the toilet.

With our bladders empty and tears wiped away and our tattered coats buttoned up (where they weren't missing buttons) it was finally time to leave.

ELEVEN

We filed out of the community centre hoping to find Sally alive upon our return. We walked along the deserted mid-day High Street in silence. There wasn't anything to talk about. Each one of us remained lost in our own thoughts.

We've all made numerous trips to the STD clinic in our miserable lives. Not because we had husbands who fucked the sectary on the side like normal people but to be tested after some fat sweaty cock-sucker blew his load in us even after we forcibly told him to "fuck off". It was a common occurrence but once Rae was gone we were confident that it would happen less and less.

We knew exactly where we were going. Sounds of pleasure danced on the frosty winter air. Unfortunately, our medication-addled minds didn't think to bring something with us that could be used to bash the doctor over the head. We had them trapped in the back alley.

The doctor was too concerned with making notes on the diseases as they entered his body to notice the likes of us. Rae noticed us. She heard our clumsy footsteps. She must have thought we wanted to join her because that's what she always thought. As it was, she made no effort to escape.

Looking at us in our ragged clothing with missing teeth, she mustn't have wanted us to join in and make it an orgy. But, then again, Rae doesn't have any standards. Even with our menacing expressions, or as menacing as middle age heavily medicated woman can muster, she didn't realise that she was in danger. Her doctor still hadn't noticed, even though he would have caught a whiff of our interesting smells by that point.

Rae impaled herself further on the cock between her legs. She was trying to feel something which must be a difficult task for someone that loose. Whether or not she was laying claim to him or trying to entice us we'll never know or care.

Rae had nowhere to go when we reached for her. It was the first time she noticed ill-feelings directed at her. The crumbling bricks couldn't support her immense arse. She let out a yelp like a puppy being kicked but puppies, even abused ones, are cute – she on the other hand, was a hideous beast of a woman. Perhaps she actually was frightened but the explanation that rang most true was that it was an attempt to manipulate with a failed attempt at cuteness.

No one wanted to touch Rae for fear of picking up some awful incurable untreatable disease. But in order to return with her we had to. Those of us with gloves or socks on our hands were the ones unlucky enough to grab her and pry her away for the cock. No one bothered to pull up her trousers, allowing the rotten smell of fish to penetrate the air – at the very least this smell would keep the unfriendly PO off our backs. No one wanted to risk getting that close to her arse and vagina; tentacles might sweep out and suck us in, breaking us down with vagina fluid the strength of stomach acid. In that particular town, walking around with trousers around ones ankles in the middle of winter was hardly an uncommon sight.

We left the doctor in the cold alley with a leaking erection. He wasn't our concern. Besides, he really shouldn't be trying to personally experience various sexually transmitted diseases by catching them first hand from one of his patients. Even in a sick world that stands out.

Rae didn't struggle. She looked sufficiently helpless, but it was hopeless. It would have been easier for her to catch the attention of a knight in shining armour being helpless, but no knights came to Rae's rescue. Not even a toothless junkie with track marks all over his withered cock and under his dirty toenails, enquired about her safety.

Rae was on her own and under our control. It looks like the sun does shine on both sinners and saints alike.

At that moment none of us knew which camp we belonged to. That would have required more brain power than any of us could have mustered.

TWELVE

The other support groups paid no attention to us as we dragged Rae back to our room. We thought she would put up a fight but she didn't, which was actually rather disappointing. We didn't need to tie her up or gag her. This town lacks knights of any variety.

Sally glanced at her. The fever reducing painkillers had obviously hit her system while we were away. Tea and stale biscuits appeared. Maria must have supplied both.

Maria's fists clenched and her eyes narrowed at the sight of Rae, unlike Sally's. There would be time to use Rae as a punching bag after her date with the fishes.

No matter what we could do to her, it would never make up for what torments we've experienced at the fault of Rae.

We weren't sure if she'd run if we let our guard down so we didn't, even as we drank our weak tea and ate our stale biscuits. Rae's big blue eyes stared up at us looking for mercy. She wasn't about to be given any.

There wasn't a spare plastic chair so we forced her to the floor. Her pants and trousers were still around her ankles. Toxic ooze seeped out of her crevices and burned through the tiles. It didn't smoulder enough to set off the smoke alarms. It wasn't our fault she didn't have enough intelligence to pull them up without being told.

She didn't say anything. Rae didn't even enquire about why she was taken out of the alley and away from her doctor friend. She didn't have the slight bit of curiosity directed towards us. She was a strange loathsome creature. She didn't ask whether we meant to cause her harm.

Debbie took it upon herself to explain but the language used was far too complex for Rae's feeble mind. She should have told it like a fairy tale for young girls but Debbie had never had the opportunity to read children's fairy tale books as an adult and the medication wiped away her early memories.

The other explanation for Rae not expressing any form of comprehension was she was too busy fantasising about Prince Charming coming along to rescue her on a white stallion. He'd have a sword in his hand that would reflect the fluorescents overhead to slay us foul beasts.

Such a sickening thought, yet, this was what Rae had come to expect from those around her, especially the part of the population who had penises. Even if she was able to draw the attention of six of the sheep hoarders and seven of the kleptomaniacs, they weren't going to rescue her – they weren't happy about the diseases Rae shared with them. In fact, three of them had sat in on a few of our support group sessions before going back to their own with the realisation that the diseases eat through latex so even protected sex with Rae remained impossible and masturbation caused second degree burns to their hands.

Once we were done with her, it never being our intention to kill her, we planned to offer her to the other support groups. We were going to charge a small fee so we could buy ourselves some fresh biscuits. We needed to keep her alive to inflict enough pain upon her to exact suitable vengeance. Anyone renting her from that point would have to sign a contract promising they weren't going to kill Rae outright. We needed to keep her alive so we could inflict maximum pain over a prolonged timespan. Pain wouldn't bring back anyone's children, nor would it stop all the rapes but it was a nice place to start.

THIRTEEN

With our cups stacked on the draining board in the shared kitchen we stripped Rae's clothing and let the cold dance goosepimples across her pale flesh and into the stretchmarks, which were an odd shade of green. We think it was body paint but no one was prepared to wipe at it and find out. Her nakedness would have been vomit-inducing but we swallowed it down as we weren't sure if we'd be allowed another meal that day.

She didn't resist the forcible removal of her clothing but we didn't expect her too. Why would she? She hadn't put up any sort of a fight before; Prince Charming was never far away. We knew she had a preference for grossing out the public by wearing as little or no clothes whenever possible. We believed she enjoyed nudity and the way the cold air touched her skin.

We decided to bind her wrists and ankles with the razor wire. We wanted to cause pain but we also wanted to witness a reaction. Apart from manipulation, we weren't sure Rae was capable of reacting to anything.

We looked for the subtle signs we knew men wouldn't be immune to no matter how grotesque the one sending the signals was. Sure enough, they were there. Whether it was an automatic reflex after years of wrapping people around her bloated finger or if she was putting conscious effort into it we didn't know, nor did we care. Nothing she could do or say would stop us from giving her what she deserved. Her attempted manipulation only furthered our revulsion.

We know she felt the razor wire digging into her flesh. We watched the blood drip. It wouldn't be surprising if we would have found her vagina in a state of gooey wetness but no one wanted to risk their fingers being sucked into that black hole. Not to mention, her secretions were toxic.

We found disappointment in that she seemed to be getting off, but the reality of the situation was one each of us expected. At least Rae wasn't vocal in her attempts to bring would-be rescuers to her aide.

FOURTEEN

Edie opened the packet of flexi-straws. Rae showed no reaction, not even when three were shoved into each nostril. A fourth would have fit but we wanted to save room for fish to swim into her brain. We didn't put any in her mouth. We would need to ensure she breathed through her piggy-nose. And we weren't really going to drown her like she has done to so many infants. That would be far too easy and we desired hiding her from death for a while – long enough to make her suffer and pay her debts, which would far exceed our lifetimes.

Rae didn't seem to notice the fish tank until her lank blonde locks were submerged in the festering water. It was a tough decision picking the unlucky ladies to dunk her head in. Everyone wanted to torture her; but no one wanted to touch her.

Her flesh was cold and clammy and covered in disease. It was possible to see the bacteria colonies growing on her skin as they battled with one another like warring nations without a microscope or even a magnifying glass (not like we would ever be allowed either).

In the end, we all decided to touch her to make it fair. All except Sally. She didn't know what was happening, where she was or even who she was.

We hoped Sally would regain consciousness at some point. Sally needed to see Rae pay.

We pushed her head under water and held her there with hopes that she was inhaling fish, both living and dead. Then we pulled her out. Maria punched her eyes before we submerged Rae's ugly head again. We don't know how long we continued like that or how many of Rae's bruises were acquired each time we pulled her out. Waterboarding, however, even in a tank of dying fish bloated off the crusty feet of the town's hookers, was not repayment enough for Rae's sins. Each of us took a turn kicking her after the final dunk. We were tired, strung out on adrenaline and wet but not finished.

We had to restrain Lisa from jumping on Rae and killing her there and then. It wasn't the right time, not when we had so much more of that sort planned for her. The images were dancing behind a curtain in our heads but weren't yet revealed to us. The thought and the motive were there; the important things.

'RAE'~Dani Brown~

Lisa settled for kicking Rae. We heard a crack which we could only assume were her ribs breaking. We waited with baited breath to see if she would cough up blood. She didn't. It wasn't time for punctured lungs so it came as a relief.

Edie caught a half dead fish in her hand while Lucy ripped the straws out of Rae's nostrils. Her beady eyes darted back and forth. Clearly, we were having an impact on her mental state.

The little fish put on a feeble display of squirming. Medication had dulled our sense of empathy, even for the smallest most pathetic of creatures. It was shoved up Rae's nose with no ceremony. A bit of nose candy for any of Rae's drowned infants that had to suffer an hour of the agony of cocaine withdrawal while Rae or a male associate stitched her up. Edie scooped up another fish. The plan was to shove Rae's oversized piggy nostrils full of half-dead pedicure fish before making her swallow the dead ones. And that's exactly what we did.

Rae's submissive lack of protest pissed us off. Even with her wrists and ankles bound she should have fought back or offered a resemblance of doing so. It should have been obvious by that point that knights in shining armour did not exist. Debbie even said as much but Rae's only reaction outside of her feeble attempts at manipulation were her eyes darting back and forth like she was trapped in the rapid eye movement stage of the sleep cycle.

She didn't even gag on the dead fish, let alone turn her head away when we held a glass filled with them and a little festering water to her lips. We didn't need to massage her throat and pinch her piggy nose to make her swallow them down; come to think of it, she's swallowed down much worse than a pint of dead fish.

Rae sat naked in the middle of our floor awaiting our next move as Sally collapsed out of her plastic seat. We knew an ambulance wouldn't come for Sally, even with Rae in our custody and therefore unable to wreak havoc. An ambulance might have come for Rae though, with all the problems and destruction, if Rae was unwell she was entitled to medical treatment, unlike Sally.

FIFTEEN

Sally had one last moment of clarity and strength. We handed her a broom. We didn't have a cricket bat wrapped with razor wire, a fact which caused regret on our part. If we had known Sally wasn't going to survive the hour we would have ensured we had one even if we had to risk arrest by stealing it from the sports shop. The broom handle was wooden and splintery. Sally put it to good use in Rae's gaping vagina. Unfortunately the toxic secretions ate through it but there was still enough handle left to get to work on her anus. Sally then had the genius idea of pouring boiling weak tea and UHT milk into Rae's arse.

We weren't sure if Rae was expressing pain or not. We hoped so. Even someone with holes as big as hers would fail to feel a splintery bit of wood. The rough way Sally controlled the broom handle would have hit against her vaginal and anal walls.

Cocks can be bendy and flexible, broom handles, less so. Rae's face contorted. We could only hope from pain but she could have experienced an orgasm. If our experiences of snuggling with a struggle from Rae's rejected suitors were anything to go by, Rae liked it rough.

We didn't tell Sally that she might be causing Rae pleasure instead of the intended pain. We didn't want to take the moment away from her. She moved in a way that suggested she wasn't in pain any more but that was impossible, the bruises hadn't even faded yet to yellow.

Sally swirled the tea and UHT milk around in Rae's anus with the broom handle. She didn't risk putting it back in Rae's vagina to be eaten by toxic secretions. The velocity of the attack was lost as fever swept through Sally's body and delirium took over.

The broom handle fell away. Sally collapsed to the floor. Rae showed no signs of relief. She looked doe-eyed at the floor, never looking up at any of us or even investigating Sally with her beady eyes, in a state of rest from their previous darting.

The lack of interest in Sally further pissed us off. Rae's sluttish ways caused Sally to be attacked in the cinema. Rae's attention seeking meant it was Sally that had to go without the much needed medical intervention. Sally's demise was purely the fault of Rae in a round-a-bout sort of way.

We didn't have time to mourn the loss of our friend. We had to clear out of the community centre by a certain time each evening, otherwise we would attract attention. That evening was not a night we wanted to do that. Not with Rae in our custody.

We didn't have much clue about what to do with Sally's body. We didn't think an ambulance would come out. If one did arrive we would have been discovered with Rae. She probably infected the paramedics with a flesh eating cousin of lymphogranuloma venereum. They're probably disappointed she didn't give them antibiotic resistant gonorrhoea and will rescue her to catch the disease.

We decided it might be best to store Sally's body in the cupboard with the broom handle and dusty mops while Rae remains in our custody. The cleaners use the main cupboard. We can only hope they never look in the one in our room. Locking it would prove too suspicious.

We wanted to give Sally more dignity but that just wasn't possible. Our meds dulled our emotions so we didn't dwell on her death or unceremonious body storage overly much.

SIXTEEN

We decided to make Rae drink all the fish and festering water while we pondered our next move. Our heavily medicated existence did not make this easy. Our thought processes were slowed as a result of the various prescriptions.

Half a day of torture wasn't enough to repay her debts; it was more like a phone call to the debt collection agency to hack out a repayment schedule. Having just laid Sally to rest in the cupboard, we decided we could leave Rae with her overnight. But we still had a few more hours before we would be allowed into our accommodation.

Her submissiveness was infuriating. Each of us kicked her at least once. We had to be careful to not stamp on her head. We needed her alive. Crushing her skull was too risky.

Lisa wanted to perform surgery on her. Lisa had dreams of becoming a surgeon before Rae's actions determined Lisa was too stupid for such a thing. She kept a rusty old hobby knife and even a few spare blades beneath the loose tiles. It didn't matter it wasn't sterile and a bit dull. It would leave Rae with re-arranged bowels and a blossoming infection.

We decided the first incisions could be made before going home. That way they could fester overnight as Sally's body entered rigor mortis. The fish left in Rae's nostrils can be sewn into the wounds. She was too submissive and too lacking in the intelligence department to even consider cutting them out and plotting an escape.

We didn't want to risk a scream of surprise as the first cuts are made to draw the attention of the other support groups while Lisa sliced into her belly. Sally's underpants would serve as a decently poetic gag.

Sally's body was still warm in the broom cupboard. She was bloated with the first signs of decay. We don't want to be around when those gases are released. Rae will be locked in the cupboard with her. It has a little ventilation grill so she'll have all the benefits of the bad odours without the suffocation.

Debbie was the unfortunate soul to do the actual removing. Only one of us would fit in the cupboard. She reached in for the tights. She informed us of the bruising and pus that had fused them to Sally's skin. Debbie threw them out of the cupboard. They were filthy. If Sally's crusty panties weren't enough of a gag we had the option of her tights.

Lucy kicked Rae's ribs on the side that wasn't broken when she saw the state of the tights. A few fish leaked out of her nostrils with the force but that didn't matter as they were soon to be sewn into her gut. A little floor dust and dirt would be good for them, or good for increasing the probability of an overnight fast-acting and painful infection.

Debbie came out of the closet close to vomiting. The cupboard must have stunk of early decomposition and late sickness, even with the door open. She needed some fresh air before she could get the crusty panties. She wiped her hands on her trousers without realising what she was doing. With her hands now pus-free, Debbie went in for Sally's pants.

Rae looked at the tights lying in pus-splatter. She was stupid but it was doubtful she was stupid enough to not realise the purpose behind stripping Sally's body of her undergarments. Her eyes grew wider than they were already. She was probably trying to think up some new way to manipulate herself into a different gag – perhaps a nice new one from the bondage section of the sex shop.

Sally's crusty knickers were going to be her gag no matter what she did. If it weren't for Rae, Sally's chances of a bruised and festering vagina would have decreased while her chance of continued life increased.

Maybe Rae thought she could make herself look cute like a Japanese princess with unnatural blonde hair and that would win us over. It worked on every man she came into contact with. What she didn't realise, or pretend not to realise was men only enjoyed her company because she was an easy submissive slut without a mind of her own. Lucy kicked her yet again. The whimpers echoed around the room.

Rae's naked flesh was enough to give us all nightmares that night. We weren't sure what was worse: dragging Sally's cooling corpse to the disused broom cupboard or the sight of Rae's cellulite.

The odours wafting through the air in our room that late afternoon were enough to convince us that a sewage treatment plant would smell like a countryside flower garden in late spring in comparison. Poor Debbie had the worst of it being that close to Sally in such confined quarters. No one had any vapour rub or flavoured lip gloss to dull the scent. Both were out of our price range and even if they weren't we probably wouldn't have been trusted with them. There was air freshener in the toilets. It was cheap but it might serve to mask the odour coming from the broom cupboard and prevent overnight investigation.

The rest of us imagined Debbie as she stuck her fingers into the waistband of Sally's lacy pound shop knickers – we were in this together, even if we couldn't witness the act itself. Our imaginations weren't that strong. Years of medications had rendered them virtually useless. We had enough left to realise the pants were going to be difficult to remove. Apart from Sally's dead weight and gas filling body, the pus, piss and shit had glued the cheap fabric to her body and the bruising poked through the holes in the flower design.

Rae stared at the tights. We didn't think she was stupid enough to not know what was coming next but years of feigning helplessness can do weird things to one's mind. Years of playing the dumb princess could have made her into one.

We didn't want to draw any attention to ourselves; we couldn't risk discovery. Attention seeking was a hobby of Rae's but so was submission like the perfect little (read: obese) princess so we couldn't be sure what she would do if she figured it out. So far, she seemed happy to submit to us whilst trying to play her pathetic mind games. When she finally worked out that manipulating us was pointless we didn't know how she would react.

Quickness was required but the body fluids served as superglue. Sally hadn't reached the stage were the building gases would be released and possibly loosen the pus and shit. Unless it was possible to offer help from beyond the grave, we weren't getting any. Even cotton underwear would have stuck. Plain cotton was far outside of our price range even in the case of a medical emergency. It might have been more comfortable and much easier to peel away than the pound shop monstrosity she was wearing.

Lucy went to help Debbie with the task. It must have been a tight squeeze in the cupboard with all the old dusty mops. The rest of us guarded Rae ready to pounce at the slightest indication of attention seeking or advanced manipulation. We needn't have worried; Rae may have been manipulative but she lacked the intelligence to become a master.

We didn't think Rae had a soul. Her lack of intellect in a disorder characterised by intelligence meant she couldn't be called a sociopath on a technicality. A more intelligent manipulative attention seeker would have feigned post-traumatic stress. It was our intention to give her the genuine disorder.

Rae appeared bored watching blood drip out of her wrists and ankles. She was thinking of how she could make it look like a suicide attempt for more sympathy from her suitors. We could just about hear their voices in our heads telling her how she has so much to live for. It was pathetic.

Rae didn't squirm as much as we had hoped. It came across like she was indifferent about the razor wire digging into her. Any of us would have been crying with the pain of having skin scraped away while it cut deeper into our flesh.

The razor wire wasn't as sharp as we thought it would be. We greeted that with only mild disappointment. Even if medication hadn't dulled our emotions, mild was all it would be. If Rae was to bleed out through her wrists and ankles it would prevent further payback. The scratches it caused could only be seen as a cry for attention by her suitors instead of an actual suicide attempt. The cuts were deep enough to draw small amounts of blood and let in an infection. We simply wanted it to be more painful for her.

We only planned on making a shallow incision into her stomach. The disembowelment or partial disembowelment wasn't scheduled until the next day due to the increased risk of death. We were hoping to hang her by her entrails if she remained conscious.

Debbie asked for scissors. She didn't want to dull the hobby knife and rusty extra knives further by using them to cut fabric. We weren't allowed them, or even nail cutters. No matter how hard we tried, we couldn't think of anything sinister to do with nail cutters.

Maria found a knife lying on the pavement a month ago. We hid it beneath a loose tile in the far corner of our room because it was so dusty we didn't think it had ever met with a cleaner's mop. If we had cleaning jobs we would have found it but no one wants to employ the likes of us. We weren't sure if it would slice through the synthetic fabric of Sally's knickers. We had never tested it due to the increased price of tomatoes and no one in this god-forsaken town having a heated green house in which we could steal some from.

Debbie and Lucy tried but the serrated blade was better for meat. Even if she could cut the sides away there was still the matter of peeling them off Sally's injuries and cooling corpse. She put the knife down and went back to her efforts of removing Sally's pants with her fingers. She grunted with absolute disgust. Lucy was too busy gagging to offer much help.

We wished there was a pair of latex gloves to offer Debbie. Sally's assailants would have engaged in intercourse with Rae two weeks before the assault giving ample time for 'blue waffle' to multiply in their system and become contagious before passing it onto Sally. We weren't sure how exactly this disease spread but it didn't seem fair for Debbie to take the risk of skin to skin contact with only a pair of cheap winter gloves as a barrier.

Debbie had the strongest stomach out of any us but even she was grunting at the sight and smell of Sally's injuries. The sounds were becoming louder. We grew a bit worried about attracting the attention of the other support groups. The confined space of the broom cupboard with Lucy crowding over her didn't help in this matter.

The bruises grew around and pushed through the holes in the cheap pound shop lace. We weren't sure when the last time Sally had been able to pull them down to use the toilet. We also weren't sure what the early stages of decomposition were doing to Sally's body in relation to the lacy pound shop panties.

Debbie tried to keep the knickers in one piece for reasons unknown to the rest of us, unless it was simple habit. Lucy didn't care. She took over and ripped them off while she swallowed down her vomit. That was the only way they were going to come off. It's not like Sally noticed unless her ghost sulked around in our room too frightened to pass into the afterlife in case that too was populated by people preventing her from getting on with it due to the Rae-effect.

The stench in the room became worse as more of Sally's decaying flesh was exposed. Debbie slammed the broom cupboard door shut. We were frightened the smell would seep out and alert the other support groups. We would have opened a window but some idiot had painted them shut (possibly because the sort of people who used the community centre couldn't be trusted).

SEVENTEEN

Edie pulled her ragged tee-shirt over her mouth and nose and went in to examine the body. Sally's vagina and anus oozed with a river of pus. Edie gathered some up in the lid of a jar. The stuff smelled foul. It was the perfect way to ensure Rae developed an overnight infection. We set it aside to sew into the incision in Rae's belly with the dead fish.

Debbie carried the pants between her index finger and thumb like they were contagious. Dried pus fell away like snowflakes to reveal slush beneath. If the lacy pound shop panties weren't carrying whatever Sally's assailants passed on then there was the oozing pus. That was sure to cause a nasty throat infection. At the very least it was going to leave Rae with a nasty taste to contemplate all night.

Maria demanded Rae to open her mouth, like a good sub, she obeyed. We failed to notice she had chewed the dead fish and kept the goo stored in her mouth. It showed a rare glimpse of insight on her part. She let it ooze down her chin. We didn't care, as long as there was enough space for Sally's crusty panties without Rae choking.

Debbie waited. It didn't seem possible for more revulsion to find its way etched onto her face but somehow it happened. We wished for a tooth brush to aid the chewed fish out. We were running short on time and still had minor surgery to perform. The chewed fish were probably Rae upping her efforts of manipulation or a possible demand for punishment.

Debbie shoved Sally's festering pants into Rae's mouth. She looked ready to gag but like a good submissive princess she took it. She didn't indicate that she wanted to spit them out but we wanted something to keep them secure anyways. Rae was not one to be trusted.

We wished we had some duct tape. The sheep hoarders kept some in their room for tying up sheep stolen from farmers in Wales. Tessa would sometimes talk to them. One of them wanted to court her even though the romance would be forbidden, unless a social worker found it to be cute. It would never be allowed to progress beyond the hand-holding stage.

Opening the door was a great risk. The stench was certain to seep out and make members of the other groups vomit. We decided to take it, mainly because no one wanted to put their hand over Rae's mouth to ensure she didn't spit out the pants. We heard she bites. Her fangs would be able to pass on whatever diseases she carried – these were numerous and sometimes they mated and produced new hybrid diseases. And, of course, we wanted to leave the panties in there all night to stifle any screams once we left for an anxious evening and sleepless night in our crappy homes.

Tessa opened the door the bare minimum she needed to squeeze through and left in search of tape before the smell could escape the room. Rae didn't even watch her leave. We found it tempting to kick her some more but managed to resist. She showed no signs of spitting out the crusty knickers.

The only sound to be heard in our room was Rae's heavy inhales through her over-sized nose. Nostril breathing should come easy to someone who spent so much time with a cock tickling her throat. There wasn't enough chewed fish ooze to plop onto the floor.

Tessa arrived back in the room being sure to open and close the door with speed. She wore the silver tape around her skinny wrist like a bracelet. It was the only bracelet her wrist would ever see unless she befriended the kleptomaniacs. They would steal one for her and anyone else.

Rae was lost in her own thoughts of Prince Charming and knights on white stallions. We don't think she was aware of the crusty panties in her mouth and the fish guts dripping down her chin.

Tessa approached while ripping off a piece of tape. She struggled with it. Debbie ended up taking the knife to it. None of us had the strength to rip tape, not on our diets. The knife was reluctant at first but Debbie didn't give up and won in the end. Rae didn't notice all this effort we were going through just for her.

She only glanced up as the tape went over her mouth before returning to her thoughts. Maybe detachment was her way to deal with the physical pain. She could have been thinking about some super-manipulative way to attempt escape but it seemed doubtful. All her previous attempts failed on us. She must realise if she tried again, it would only make things worse for her.

EIGHTEEN

It was Lisa's time to shine. It was time for her to prove to the world what a good surgeon she would have made if she was allowed the chance. Her rusty hobby knife was already in her hand. She carried the spare blades in their plastic case in the other hand. She had waited her entire life for this one moment.

She didn't care that her intense and obsessive anatomical knowledge was being used to induce an infection and suffering. At that point it didn't matter. Besides, we could argue that inducing an infection in the body of this one submissive princess was for the greater good.

The rest of us thought her hands might shake with the excitement but they didn't. The medication she was on dulled her to the point that she couldn't feel anything. This should have been the defining moment of Lisa's life and she stumbled along like the walking dead.

The blade slid into Rae's naked flab with ease. Lisa's hand was steady. We were expecting it to be dull because of all the rust. There was a lot of fat to slice through. Rae would sometimes let her suitors fuck her rolls if her other holes were occupied.

She put up a measly protest. We were concerned about the razor wire cutting Lisa but she didn't come close. The attempt at resistance was one of the most pathetic things any of us had ever witnessed.

A gurgling from Rae's throat echoed around the room. We could only hope she wasn't trying to suck down Sally's crusty panties to choke or scream. Silent tears cascaded down her cheeks. We thought they might actually be real. Having your belly sliced open mustn't be a pleasant feeling, especially when a few layers of fat are involved.

'RAE'~Dani Brown~

Lisa didn't need to cut as deep as she did. She didn't want to risk the dead fish falling out overnight and wanted to ensure an infection took root. The deep cuts seemed the logical choice. Disembowelment wasn't scheduled until the next day and even then it was only to be partial. We wanted our prisoner to be kept alive.

She scooped up the fish and pushed them into the incision with a bent teaspoon. The fish must have felt cool to Rae's insides. There was always the possibility that Rae's guts were infected with sushi eating parasites. There really was no way to know all the diseases Rae carried. There just weren't names for them all even if all the medical dictionaries and the entirety of the internet were to be published in one volume.

Next, the pus to act like surgical glue. It was wet and slimy. Lisa performed the surgery in discount shop winter gloves leant to her by Tessa. It would have been quicker to scoop up the pus in a gloved finger but those weren't the sort of gloves to do that in so she had to wait for gravity to take effect.

She coughed up a big wad of phlegm and spat into the wound for good measure or her lack of patience while waiting for the pus to ooze out of the jar lid. Her part was now done. Lisa stepped away and cleaned her hobby knife before placing it back under the loose tile. They would be required the following day.

When it came time to stitch her up we let Maria take over. She was a seamstress before Rae ruined her life by sucking off her dog in full view of the uptight neighbours. Because Maria was an anxious person and Rae claimed Maria had sold her the dog for that very reason, Maria was the one to get into trouble under obscenity laws. It probably didn't help that Rae fucked the judge in the case up the arse with a strap-on.

Maria had to use fishing wire and a sewing needle as that was all we could get our hands on. Sewing needles are rather sharp. It entered the first few layers of Rae's skin with ease but the fishing wire needed something to grip. Flaky skin would only tear open if Rae moved around too much during the night. It could even fall away before we throw her in there.

Maria needed to push the needle through the fat without breaking it. Sewing needles were known to bend. If it bent too much it would be useless and we would need to secure the wound with duct tape, something we wanted to avoid as it could cause problems with the scheduled partial disembowelment.

Although time was running short Maria moved slowly. She had only one chance at this. She wanted to get it right. This was the first time she was able to sew since the unfortunate incident with her dog.

We looked on. The signs of anxiety and our next dose of meds being due hit us collectively. Debbie came close to grinding away her remaining teeth. It was a tense time for everyone except Lisa.

Her medications were too strong at too high of a dosage. It was amazing she wasn't comatose. Meds wouldn't be taken until we arrived back at our crappy homes.

The needle pushed through yellow fat and came out the other side trailing the fishing wire. Maria pushed it back in. It wasn't precise; time was limited and it didn't need to be a work of art. Stitching through fat was never going to be an easy task even with a better needle. Real surgeons had staples for these sorts of wounds. Maria's wrist was aching. It clicked each time she pushed the needle into Rae's flesh.

Fishing wire was much stronger than cotton. If Maria could stitch the wound together without the needle bending the chances of the fish, pus and Lisa's chunk of phlegm leaking out through broken stitches were minimal. The infection needed time to grow and develop. Good stitching would ensure this.

It was late. We heard the other support groups vacate their rooms and the building as Maria stitched up Rae's abdomen. There was the possibility that the sheep hoarders would knock on our door asking for their tape back. Evidence of Rae needed to be in the broom cupboard by that time.

Confidence bloomed from Maria as she closed Rae up. The sewing became more precise. When she asked for the knife to break the wire the line was straight. She had even doubled back on it to ensure nothing would leak out in the night. The fish could finish the decomposition process inside Rae.

NINETEEN

Rae didn't put up a struggle as we dragged her towards the broom cupboard until she noticed Sally's body. She objected to being near a corpse. If her suitors hadn't assaulted Sally then Sally would still be alive and therefore Rae wouldn't be spending the night next to a dead body. We explained this to her but we don't think she understood.

The razor wire cut further into her wrists and ankles during her struggles. We could only hope that infection would enter those wounds too. And she wouldn't sever an artery and bleed out.

Her throat emitted a low growl. She might have been trying to argue her case. It didn't matter. She was being left over night with Sally and we weren't about to take the crusty panties out to let Rae speak. We were quite sure we wouldn't be able to get them back in again.

Her pupils went wide to the point her blue eyes were nearly black. She was used to getting her way. Everyone she had met before us had always given in to her manipulation. It was a frightening prospect for Rae. We were glad.

We threw her on top of Sally's body. Wherever Sally was, we were sure she would appreciate her grave gases escaping onto Rae during the night. Rae, however, didn't appreciate it. As soon as we shut the door she slammed herself against it. She might have been trying to plead with us to let her go or draw attention to herself for rescue or even make a feeble attempt at escape.

We should have drugged her first to ensure she wouldn't be heard but we didn't anticipate her fear of a dead body. She had murdered so many infants that she should be used to being around death but in Rae's warped mind infants were only dolls. Dolls couldn't die.

Her mouth was no longer open. We weren't going to risk removing the duct tape to slip in something to dissolve on top of the crusty knickers and maybe enter Rae's blood stream. Her vaginal secretions left a sizzling hole in the tiles so that was out of the question. None of us had the desire to die in a bath of toxic vagina juice. But we could shove a bunch of pills up her arse as suppositories with a flexistraw. That was the logical solution to the problem and the smart choice – the safe choice.

We didn't have time to waste drawing straws to decide who would be the unlucky one to get close to Rae's anus. Debbie had removed Sally's pants. Lucy helped. Lisa performed the surgery. Maria stitched her up. It was Edie's turn to do something traumatising.

We left Rae to bang against the door while we rummaged for tablets. We hoped what we came up with wouldn't react against one another and kill Rae in the night but we didn't have the brain power to think it through even with our medication wearing off.

We stood by the door ready to catch Rae if she tried to escape. It would take a few of us to pin her down all while avoiding her toxic secretions and razor wire. Edie stood ready with pills in one hand and a flexistraw in the other.

We opened the door. Rae fell out of the cupboard but didn't make any effort to move once she was away from Sally's body. She seemed to have a legitimate fear of the dead. The perfect submissive princess wouldn't make an escape attempt.

Avoiding the toxic vaginal secretions we twisted her body around until her anus was in the air. Edie wasted no time. She wanted the task done and over with. A lot vomit escaped her mouth and fell onto Rae's backside while she was shoving pill after pill up her arse with a flexistraw. Rae didn't feel it but she wouldn't with an anus that loose. It knew too many cocks.

While the pills took effect we left Rae on the floor and piled her clothes into the fish tank. It was Tessa's turn to go into the cupboard. Sally would appreciate her grave gases leaking onto Rae in the night; she wouldn't appreciate a fish tank being on top of her and wasting the precious decay. We should have really thought to hide the evidence before we bundled Rae into the broom cupboard the first time but excessive prescriptions left us in a continuous daze.

Rae's body showed signs of limpness. Being that close to a dead body she wouldn't have been able to relax into that state naturally even in an attempt to manipulate. She wouldn't notice where she was until the drugs wore off. We hoped they'd still be in effect the next morning but we planned to arrive early just in case they were wearing off by then. They should last until the cleaners were done tonight at the very least.

Even with all her fat in the heavily drugged state she was lighter and much easier to manoeuvre. We checked to make sure her nose was clear and left her there.

In our efforts to tidy up we realised nothing could be done about the floor tiles. Rae's juices had burnt holes to the concrete below. We hoped our weak tea and UHT milk wouldn't be taken away as a result. None of us had toxic vaginal secretions, even after being forced into sex acts with Rae's fucked rejects.

We needn't have worried about the sheep hoarders. They left fifteen minutes before we filed into the toilet to pee and wash away Rae's diseases. It was possible they heard all the commotion but it was obvious that we were up to something anyways. They didn't seem interested. They were probably more concerned with their weekend trip to Wales for more sheep.

TWENTY

As promised, the next morning we arrived early. We were the first support group there. We didn't even stop to put on the kettle. We ran straight to the broom cupboard and opened the door. Rae was in a state. The drugs had worn off. She was shaking with fear and hot with fever. This was exactly how we wanted to find her. If she made any attempt to alert someone to her being in there she failed.

Debbie put the kettle on after viewing Rae. Edie helped with the tea. The rest of us pulled Rae out of the broom cupboard and shut the door before the smell could escape to the rest of the community centre and its source investigated. Sally's body sighed. We needed to trap the gas inside before it alerted anyone to the fact we have a dead body in here along with Rae.

Lucy stole the cheap air freshener from the toilets. It was possible the junkie cleaners used most of it to get high but there was a little left in the can. A little was better than nothing when it came to masking the scent of decay and Rae. They'd be upset there was none left for them that evening but masking the stench was more important than the feelings and withdrawals of addicts.

We weren't sure what support group arrived first or what time they would show up. This was the first time we were in the community centre before anyone else. We had extra meds incase Rae put up a struggle during the partial disembowelment. We didn't think she would. It was the hanging her with her own entrails part we were concerned about. The only place to do that was in the broom cupboard with Sally's body. Rae might put up a struggle then. We didn't want her actually hanging herself or fully disembowelling herself – either would kill her. It wouldn't be time for her date with the Grim Reaper for quite a while yet.

We dragged Rae to the centre of the room and parked her on top of the tiles her secretions burnt through. We arranged our chairs around her. Debbie and Edie handed out weak teas. We studied Rae's body for red marks of spreading infection while we drank the first cup.

Her wrists were shredded from the razor wire, as were her ankles. The abdominal incision was bright pink with tentacles spreading out across her belly and down towards her groin. Our eyes didn't want to travel further south. Her flesh had given us all a night filled with bad dreams, even Lisa with double the amount of prescriptions as the rest of us.

Rae's vagina was already host to mutant variants of sexually transmitted diseases. It wasn't necessary to find out if the infection from the dead fish, pus and spit had spread that low. If her secretions burnt through more tiles in the first half of the day then we would know. She must have extra drippings from all the shaking.

We weren't sure if Rae knew where she was. It took days of awareness before the infection took Sally. We hoped it would the same for Rae. But Sally was a fighter; Rae was a pathetic princess waiting for Prince Charming.

She pissed herself in the night. That was to be expected. She drank a lot of festering water. Fortunately she didn't shit herself. She could have lost the pills if she did. She wasn't aware that she was perfumed with the strong scent of stale urine. It masked the woke-up-next-to-a-corpse smell nicely.

Once our first cup of tea was finished, Maria and Lisa set to undoing the fishing wire. Pus had seeped out. The rest of us were left to either watch or brew a second cup. Lisa's hobby knife was more up to the task than anything else.

The smell was intense with the stitching gone and the wound left open. We didn't realise it was possible for that much pus to appear overnight. We wished we had a hoover to suction it out and feed it to her for breakfast. Curiosity was the only reason we opened it, a move we regretted.

We clogged up the crack beneath the door with our coats so the arriving support groups wouldn't notice. It quickly became uncomfortable in our room. We were only slightly worried about the lack of oxygen and disease entering our respiratory systems through pus droplets carried on the air.

We thought it might be safe to remove the gag. We wanted to hear any feeble protests. Rae was in no fit state to scream for a rescuer. Her pathetic noises might sound like screams to her ears. The look we expected to see when Prince Charming didn't show up would be priceless.

Maria pulled the tape off. Rae's skin came with it. Fish goo flaked away. We expected Rae to spit out the crusty panties but she didn't. Her lack of awareness pissed us off. Debbie kicked her. The panties leaked half way out of her mouth like cheese cloth at a séance. That suited us.

TWENTY-ONE

Lisa didn't want her second cup of tea. She wanted to start the surgery right away. Less delay meant more torture. She pulled out her rusty hobby knife and cut into Rae's belly above the pus-bloated incision from the previous night. Lisa didn't want to put her hands in it.

Debbie scratched at her wrists and fingers. It wasn't the absent minded scratching of a passing itch; she really dug her claws in. The skin looked red and sore. It seeped in places where it had come up into boils. We hoped Lisa wouldn't notice, it would put her off performing the partial disembowelment and she was the only one of us to have the knowledge and know-how.

More of the crusty panty escaped Rae's mouth. She made a squeaking noise with the blade pressing into her fat. Lisa didn't notice. She was searching for her intestines.

We were aware that even a partial disembowelment had a high risk of death but it was a chance we wanted to take. If successful the pay-off would be satisfactory. Not great, our medication dulled us to the point that great couldn't be felt.

If we weren't so heavily medicated we would have been feeling rather giddy with the excitement. All except Debbie, she wasn't looking so well. Edie went to fetch another cup of tea for her.

The skin on Debbie's fingers was slipping off the small layer of fat. She didn't have finger prints any longer. Her cheeks were flushed with a developing fever. We knew it related to removing Sally's crusty pound shop knickers. We wanted to say it was worth it for the gag but we cared about Debbie and we didn't want to lose another friend to be unceremoniously disposed of in the disused broom cupboard. The boils were erupting in miniature explosions. Those of us that were sitting closest to her moved away by a few inches.

Lisa was too medicated and too intent on what she was doing to notice the commotion of cheap plastic chairs rubbing against cold tiles. The sound was loud and shrill but not as bad as nails against a chalk board.

Lisa cut through another layer of fat before she needed to change the blade on her hobby knife. She was wrist deep in Rae's belly. We knew that her hands would look like Debbie's before the next day. We didn't have any reason to live other than to seek reimbursement from Rae. If we died getting it, it wouldn't matter. It isn't like we had anyone to miss us other than each other.

A smile graced Debbie's face. She was aware of what was going on. She was going to fight to stay with us until Rae was hanging by her entrails. We wished Sally was still with us to witness it. She was with us in spirit at least.

TWENTY-TWO

Rae was picked up by the police later that day. Reports had trickled in from concerned citizens of a fat woman with cuts to her stomach wearing linked sausages around her neck. Some reports said she had a piece of clothing hanging out of her mouth; others that she was foaming at the mouth. All the reports agreed with one another about her flesh having a green tinge to it. Her choice in bracelets seemed to point towards razor wire.

At first the emergency call centre staff thought it was kids just playing a prank. That is until more calls came in from all over the town. They weren't sure if the police or ambulance would be more appropriate so they sent out both.

Rae was picked up in a salon in broad daylight. The owner squawked in some foreign language combined with broken English about the fat naked woman eating the fish out of his tank while she wiped her lips with underpants she pulled out of her throat. The ambulance crew followed behind and called for back-up – paramedics were needed to deal with the salon's traumatised clientele.

She was naked with incisions to her belly, apart from the collar around her neck and the razor wire worn around her wrists. Body paint didn't count as clothing. Neither did the big purple butt plug up her arse. She was foaming at the mouth but that could have been merely her attempt to eat her underwear or half chewed raw fish. Never the less, environmental health had to be called in case it was rabies. She had linked sausages hanging around her neck and duct tapped to her belly.

The episode was mentally scarring to anyone unfortunate enough to witness it. The arresting officers and the paramedics were all signed off from work with stress related illnesses.

Rae mumbled something about a ghost. Someone named Sally had died. Her body was stored in the broom cupboard.

TWENTY-THREE

"And that's when I realised there was never a *we* but always a *me*. In that brief moment of clarity, I knew that I had brought all this upon myself. I'm not sure if I regret it, or what it is, exactly. It was always me. No amount of dissociation will ever change that.

'RAE'~Dani Brown~

Lisa, Debbie, Lucy, Sally – they don't exist except in my imagination. It was all merely to get attention at first but over time the characters developed and took on a life of their own."

Rae stared straight ahead. Someone had the unfortunate task of washing her and dressing her. Rae, in a faraway sense, heard the caretaker as she gagged on her own vomit. Her words to the police officer were slow. It was like her vocal cords were a new and previously undiscovered part of her.

"Rae, I'm going to call the doctor back now."

The police officer stood up to leave. Her chair scraped against the cold concrete floor. Rae cringed at the sound. The police officer was more than a little unnerved by the woman. It was going to be a tough task separating fact from fiction in this case.

END.

Dani Brown, Liverpool, January–September 2014

'RAE'~Dani Brown~

ABOUT THE AUTHOR

Dani Brown spends her time drinking far too much coffee and knitting in Liverpool. Lots of people think she is much more interesting than she actually is. Her clothes are always covered in cat fur and she has a degree in creative writing from the University of Bedfordshire which is probably the two most interesting things about her (if you ignore her obsession with Mayhem's drummer – most people do).

'RAE'~Dani Brown~

Morbidbooks is a grotesque Bizarro ballet where the most profane things occur. An impious and perverse dwelling of dark revulsion. A cozy cottage where torture porn and brutal bible tales are devised. A quiet place to relax and spin tales of depravity and wickedness. A halfway house for the disturbed where rules no longer apply. A safe haven for deviant serial killers to hatch their wretched schemes.

Bring your pets.

The tasty ones are always welcome.

Morbidbooks.Wordpress.Com

'RAE'~Dani Brown~

Also available from ~MorbidbookS~

In Print & Kindle Editions:

'click' on the following book cover images for Kindle hyperlink.

'RAE'~Dani Brown~

~The hands of the girls were inside of each-others zip front grey boiler suits and they sat in the blood from where Sonny's face collided with the surface. The brunette had a finger smear of it next to her mouth.

"You two sluts put each other down and go tell Moira that Sonny's done. I'm coming in, just got a little business to attend to first."

As the two started to leave the big blond grabbed the shoulder of the red head and pulled her back.

"Not you Fire-Crotch, all this fucking blood has got me going." She started to unbuckle the belt on her camouflage hot pants. "Down you go, bitch!"

~Short stories from the Most Depraved Writer in Print. Dark and twisted tales of exquisite violence, rough tricks, narcotics consumption, evil ghosts and drug-snuffling demons. Evil grandfathers and animal-human hybrid clones. Morbid serial killer stalking night darkened hallways of an unsuspecting hospital. Life underground following the frozen apocalypse. Tales of ancient blood-thirsty vampires and Roman decadence. Enjoy all of the hardcore, dystopic, viscerally violent stories. Not for easily offended mamby-pambies. Dark fiction at its finest.

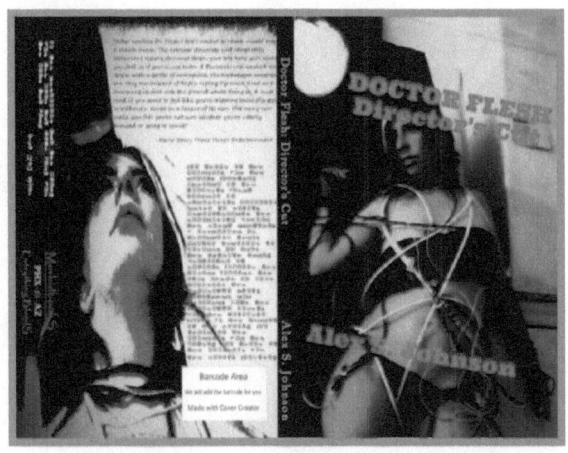

~From Alex S. Johnson, the author of **Bad Sunset,
Wicked Candy and The Death Jazz,** comes a new
vision in Bizarro horror. Imagine a TROMA film on
meth and acid, one part cyberpunk, one part Franz
Kafka, and three parts frankly unsuitable for a sane
audience. "Will make you feel as if you've just eaten 8
Percocets and washed 'em down with a bottle of
moonshine," says Necro Stein of Texas Terror
Entertainment.

'RAE'~Dani Brown~

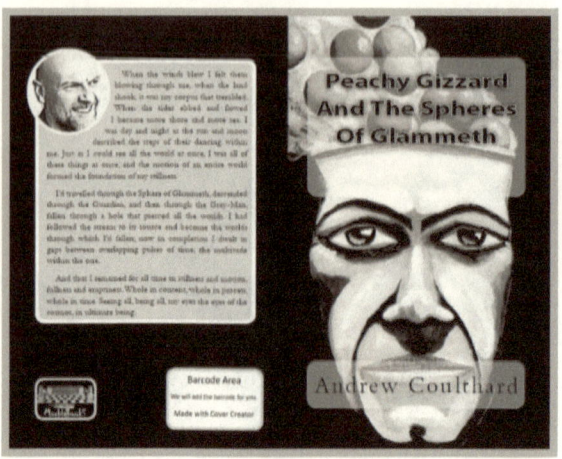

~**When the winds blew i felt them blowing through me,** when the land shook, it was my corpus that trembled. When the tides ebbed and flowed I became more shore and more sea. I was day and night as the sun and moon described the steps of their dancing within me. Just as I could see all the world at once, I was all of these things at once, and the motion of an entire world formed the foundation of my stillness. I'd travelled through the Sphere of Glammeth, descended through the Guardian, and then through the Grey-Man, fallen through a hole that pierced all the worlds.

~**He had to have her the moment he saw her trachea ring**. Six months later she was his lovely wife. He performed his duties as a husband and she as a wife. He tolerated a house filled with references to her late first husband and the children they had together. He put up with her prudish ways. He waited. He was patient. He planned. He was adaptable. He was rewarded over the course of a week in her basement. He turned his perverse sexual fantasies of worms and maggots and her lovely crusty trachea ring into a gruesome reality.

'RAE'~Dani Brown~

~A dirty shameful devil of a secret...

Something that two men share. A legacy that will shock you to your very core. One that is created not out of madness, but of the purest desire. Take a vivid journey into the mind of the killer and his biggest fan. Do you believe in evil? See the knife plunge. Lap at the wounds. Do you still? There is no rational meaning or pretty words that will hide away the darkness that the words of this found journal creates. Inside is the real truth. And it can set you free. Watch all you want. Taste what you dare not have.

'RAE'~Dani Brown~

~"The routine has this inherent tendency to perpetuate lies, and I speak only in thinly veiled euphemisms — hanging out with friends means going to the bar; being tired means too many sleepless nights on amphetamine; going grocery shopping means robbing Price Chopper blind; filling a prescription means visiting my dealer; going to the bank means pawning my possessions — but refer to them not as "lies;" rather, label them as weak excuses utilized to justify my erratic behaviours.

'RAE'~Dani Brown~

~**I'm feeling down and dirty, feeling kind of mean,** so I give those fans my middle finger. Those poor bastards go nuts. My team looks at me in awe. My coach frowns and the opposing one begins to furiously scratch out new plays. I see our opponents and I almost feel sorry for the poor bastards. Their fans can't help them. Their coach can't help them. I'm going to run them off their own track in front of their own fans and there is not one thing they can do about it.

~**Humanity is the devil is a deconstructed nightmare mixing David Lynch and snuff movies.** The plot revolves around a central character, Seth, who is set about a crusade against humanity which, for him, represents pure evil. Through random killings he and his cronies try to accelerate the end of the world, in order to provoke and defeat the Demiurge, the false God that is ruling the earth. As in Burroughs, logical language is replaced here with cut-scenes – sometimes to be taken literally – that plunge the reader into an extreme experience.

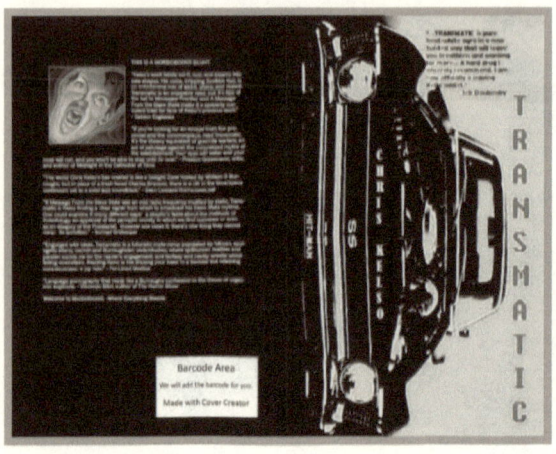

~"As a part-time hitman/ exterminator, Ignius Ellis's dream is to buy a candy-apple red Nova Supreme. In the process of trying to earn enough cash to make his dream come true he gets sucked into the rough world of Visitacion Valley, SF. When the tenants in his apartment complex reveal their various extracurricular activities this take an even more bizarre twist and Ellis soon becomes acquainted with the nightmarish Slave State dimension..."

'RAE'~Dani Brown~

~That's the last time she gets the bigger worm...
Once their flesh flakes away the angels collapse into
puddles of hissing goop and withered petals blow
into them hurried along by unseen winds. My spit
looses its sweet taste to the black flavor of ash. The
glowing birds in the bright orange sky burst into
small sparkly novas. The sky itself weeps and tears,
streaking down like a ruined painting as the dismal
grey of life wheezes back before my eyes. I don't
blink; praying silently for one last desperate
sensation of the high. Lila feels it too. She writhes on
the mattress next to me…

~Scary as ever.

He looked at her and grinned wickedly, the overcasting shadows of the outer corner of the stone wall, combined with the flickering light above them, created a deadly feature across the side of his face. He sees her lying helpless. He chuckled eerily, and instantly raised his hand. Her eyes widened to the sight of the gleaming sharp knife in his grasp. He even held it up for her to see it better.

She stared up at him and then to the knife, panting in fear. Her heart pounded throughout her body as he chuckled once more saying deeply,

"Oh excellent. I've found you . . ."

'RAE'~Dani Brown~

~**Within these twisted and perverted pages**, Johnson manages to demolish clichés with a jaded finesse that I've personally never encountered in written form. Another apparent talent is his effortless deconstruction of pop-culture allegories and references as found in his story "Vampussy." No one is safe or spared from his dagger sharp sarcasm and wit.

While not without its flaws, my appreciation for this kind of talent and voice is what made his writing so fun to read, even if he might possibly be out of his ever-loving mind.

'RAE'~Dani Brown~

~In Garrett Cook's Murderland serial killers are idolized by society. Their deeds are followed obsessively by television pundits and the adoring public. A subculture has grown up around this phenomena, called "Reap." Laws are created to allow this activity to flourish, including designated "safe zones' where killers can practice their trade without fear of persecution. Fans of the top rated serial killers celebrate each new kill on social media and television. Programs glorify their deeds.

The culture of Murderland is violent and mirrors our own violent society and its decadent obsessions.

~Born whole from the rectum of a dying patient, Morbid silently stalks the hospital's hallways, heinously dispatching the most helpless of patients and in the most painfully repulsive of manners. In the meantime, in order to pay for his family and home that includes his ghost step-father Sammy and his pet aborted fetus Chip, Westphal has to ingest mounds of dangerous narcotics to get through his night shifts. Barely hanging on to his Care Tech gig by his fingernails, the last thing Westphal needs is to be accused of Morbid's evil deeds. You, on the other hand, simply seek some solace from all Your diseases.

'RAE'~Dani Brown~

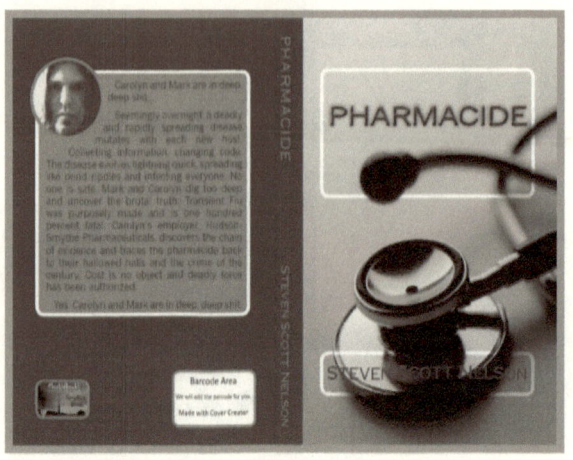

~**It looks like Carolyn and Mark are in deep, deep shit...** Mark and Carolyn live in an alternate 1989 where Ronald Reagan is on his fourth presidential term. The USA has a rigid, long-standing caste system and abortions were never made legal. Being homeless is a crime that is punishable by imprisonment in Tent City. Most of Mark's ER patients are inmates at this camp and are victims of a new disease dubbed, Transient Flu. This deadly and rapidly spreading disease mutates with each new host, collecting information, changing code. The disease evolves lightning quick, spreading like pond ripples...

'RAE'~Dani Brown~

~IMMANUEL THE CHRIST **has some nerve.** Jonah has already lost everyone he loves to Pilate the vampire and his Harbor drug violence. Jonah now trudges through his days staying as high on Plata as possible. He just wants to be left alone while he waits for his turn to die. The Christ has other plans for him. She sends Pedro, to assign Jonah to order the Herod to dismantle the Harbor's Plata trade. Jonah decides to run. But you can't run from God. As Jonah learns the hard way when the 'Edmund Fitzgerald' goes down in rough seas, with the reluctant prophet on board…

~Five Very Wicked Shorts. Brought to you with love and blood from The Grim Reverend Steven Rage, the 'Most Depraved Writer in Print'. ~

Through the sheer shock of his presentation, Rage forces readers to consider the alternatives, to look at the garbage in the streets, to see what is swept into the gutters at night right before all decent people awake to see another cleaned up version of the day. Depravity at its finest, but really the stories are loads of fun ...

~**Pontius Pilate is cursed to be a vampire**. Life after
life after life.~ And for the Plata dealing Pilate, his life
is more like a death sentence. His only chance
surviving is to keep on selling his monthly quota of
Plata. This new man-made narcotic is a potent
speed-ball designed to amp up the user, while also
numbing the conscience into euphoric oblivion. To
nullify the pain. To stifle the torture. To run and to
hid from all the anguish inside. PILATE is a drug lord
vampire in this re-telling of Christ's final days.

~So I, The Spun Monkey, have returned from running my errands, safe and sound. Having failed rehab once again, The Spun Monkey went ahead and procured myself an 8-ball of crispy, crunchy Columbian Bam-Bam. I chipped, chopped, lined and blasted off with two bigguns up each side. OOH OOH EEE EEE-fuckmerunning- OOH-OOH-OOH, motherfuckers! Monkey be ready... Yes, indeeeeeed.... Having had my jet fuel, I then sat my hairy asshole down at the keyboard and began flailing away. The monkey hopes you dig the fruits of my labors in 'The Spun Monkey's Digest'. And if you not ... well then ... you can go eff yourself, Capitan!

~Following religious folklore, parables, and beliefs,
Rage presents the readers with a God who truly is the
Shepherd that leaves no sheep behind. While this tale
is deeply woven with the intricacies of a dark, drug-
infested world ruled by evil forces, this is the story of
a lost sheep. All are God's children, even the most
foulest of evil creatures who by their own will have
become so through their spiritual and physical
copulation with the Devil, and as such, in God's
mercy, still are given a chance to be saved.

~ CARGO CONTAINS: ~

Space-wrecked on Venus by Neil R. Jones

For All the Marbles by Rev. Steven Rage

Tony and the Beetles by Philip K. Dick

Acid Bath by Vaseleos Garson

The Butterfly Kiss by Arthur Dekker Savage

The Moon Destroyers by Monroe K. Ruch

From some of the giants of the Golden Age to the darkest of dystopian noir, MorbidbookS SciFi Anthology will take you from hopeful space travel to living hand-to-mouth in the despair beneath the Earth.

Welcome to your future.

'RAE'~Dani Brown~

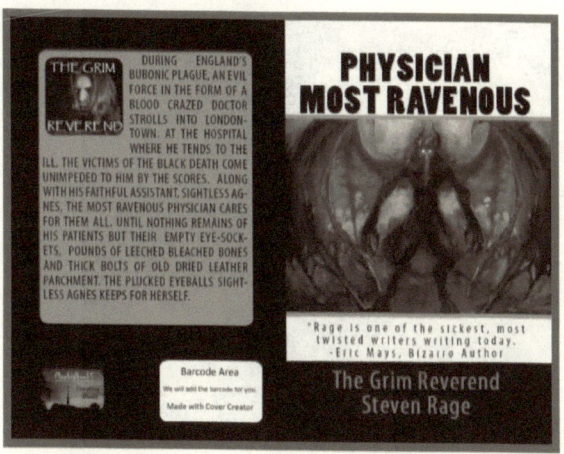

~During the height of England's Bubonic Plague an ancient Evil Force strolls into London-Town in the form of a would-be doctor. It could smell the blood from miles away, wanting only to help. At the hospital where he cares for the victims of this Black Death, the ill come to him unimpeded. They arrived and fell by the scores. With the help of his ever-faithful assistant, Sightless Agnes, a most ravenous cares for them all. Eating his way through an entire hospital, he treats them until there is nothing left. Nothing save their empty eye sockets, a few pounds of leeched bleached bones and some bolts of old dried-out flesh-leather parchment.

'RAE'~Dani Brown~

~New from MorbidbookS. Where Everything Bleeds
is an instant collector's specimen and a certain
stunner. ~ Be the first freak on your block to acquire
this singular and unexpurgated exquisite culling of
The Grim Reverend Steven Rage's favorite 'meds'.
Enjoy this one-of-a-kind vivid look into the twisted
mind of The Most Depraved Writer In Print as he
captains you through the intoxicating stain of his
wicked imagination. Included are numerous Photos,
Paintings and Illustrations embellished with dramatic
grayscale that enhance these iniquitous and
magnificent Dark Fantasy fables.

'RAE'~Dani Brown~

MorbidbookS. Everything Bleeds.

'RAF'~Dani Brown~

www.ingramcontent.com/pod-product-compliance
Lightning Source LLC
Chambersburg PA
CBHW020737130626
46554CB00006B/2032